Parents and Caregivers,

Stone Arch Readers are designed to provide enjoyable reading experiences, as well as opportunities to develop vocabulary, literacy skills, and comprehension. Here are a few ways to support your beginning reader:

- Talk with your child about the ideas addressed in the story.

- Discuss each illustration, mentioning the characters, where they are, and what they are doing.

- Read with expression, pointing to each word. You may want to read the whole story through and then revisit parts of the story to ensure that the meanings of words or phrases are understood.

- Talk about why the character did what he or she did and what your child would do in that situation.

- Help your child connect with characters and events in the story.

Remember, reading with your child should be fun, not forced. Each moment spent reading with your child is a priceless investment in his or her literacy life.

Gail Saunders-Smith, Ph.D.

Stone Arch Readers

are published by Stone Arch Books
a Capstone Imprint
1710 Roe Crest Drive
North Mankato, Minnesota 56003
www.capstonepub.com

Library of Congress Cataloging-in-Publication Data
Yasuda, Anita.
The surprise prize / by Anita Yasuda ; illustrated by Steve Harpster.
p. cm. -- (Stone Arch readers: Dino detectives)
Summary: Sara the Tryceratops has been eating Dino Delights cereal for three months and
collecting the box tops--and now she and her friends are eagerly awaiting her prize.
ISBN 978-1-4342-5969-1 (library binding) -- ISBN 978-1-4342-6198-4 (pbk.)
1. Dinosaurs--Juvenile fiction. 2. Free material--Juvenile fiction. 3. Breakfast cereals--Juvenile fiction.
[1. Dinosaurs--Fiction. 2. Free material--Fiction. 3. Breakfast cereals--Fiction.
4. Mystery and detective stories.] I. Harpster, Steve, ill. II. Title.
PZ7.Y2124Sur 2013
813.6--dc23
2012046965

Reading Consultants:
Gail Saunders-Smith, Ph.D
Melinda Melton Crow, M.Ed
Laura K. Holland, Media Specialist

Designer: Russell Griesmer

Printed in China by Nordica.
0413/CA21300422
032013
007226NORDF13

The Surprise Prize

by **Anita Yasuda**
illustrated by **Steve Harpster**

STONE ARCH BOOKS
a capstone imprint

Meet the Dino Detectives!

 Dot the
Diplodocus

 Sara the
Triceratops

 Cory the
Corythosaurus

 Ty the
T. rex

Sara loves prizes. She really wants the surprise prize from the Dino Delights cereal.

"I wonder what it is. It is a mystery!" says Sara.

She eats the cereal every morning.

Sometimes she eats it at night, too.

Sara saves all the box tops.

"What do you think the prize is?" asks Sara. "It's such a mystery!"

"Maybe it's a giant balloon!" says Dot.

"We could fly to school," says Cory.

"We could fly around town," says Ty.

"We could fly to the moon," says Sara.

"Maybe it's a boat!" says Ty.

"We could sail to school," says Cory.

"We could sail around town,"
says Dot.

"We could sail across the sea,"
says Sara.

"Maybe it's a car!" says Cory.

"We could drive to school," says Dot.

"We could drive around town," says Ty.

"We could drive in a race," says Sara.

Sara eats the cereal for two months. She finally has enough box tops.

She sends them away for the
prize. Then she waits and waits.

Finally, a delivery truck stops at Sara's house.

"My prize is here!" says Sara.

The prize is in a big box.

"I have to call my friends!"
says Sara.

Her friends rush to Sara's house.

"It's a balloon!" says Dot.

"It's a boat!" says Ty.

"It's a car!" says Cory.

Sara lifts the box. It's very light.

Sara pushes the box. It's very tall.

"I'm so excited!" says Sara.

"Open it!" her friends yell.

Sara slowly opens the box.

Sara's mystery is finally solved.
Her prize is more Dino Delights.
Boxes and boxes of them.

"Oh no!" says Sara. "I can't eat any more Dino Delights!"

"We'll eat them!" her friends say.

"Dino Delights for everyone!"
says Sara.

STORY WORDS

prizes	delights	mystery
suprise	cereal	delivery

Total Word Count: 285